Snakes

by
David Orme

Thunderbolts

Snakes
by David Orme

Illustrated by Martin Roy

Published by Ransom Publishing Ltd.
Unit 7, Brocklands Farm, West Meon, Hants. GU32 1JN, UK
www.ransom.co.uk

ISBN   978 178127 0585

First published in 2013
Reprinted 2022

Copyright © 2013 Ransom Publishing Ltd.

Illustrations copyright © 2013 Martin Roy

'Get the Facts' section - images copyright: cover, prelims, passim – Darren Patterson, Ltshears, StuPorts, Lee Daniels, seamartini; pp 4/5 - Tim Vickers; pp 8/9 - Nehrams2020, Rsduhamel, Clinton & Charles Robertson; pp 10/11 - StuPorts, Tim Vickers, Tad Arensmeier; pp 12/13 - H. Zell, Jan Rehschuh, Шатилло Г.В.; pp 14/15 - Wibowo Djatmiko; pp 16/17 - Darren Patterson, John Kirk; pp 18/19 - Hari Prasad, Dr. osh, Xavier Arnau; pp 20/21 - iSIRIPONG, Shizhao, Ltshears, Brandon Laufenberg, Linda Tanner; pp 22/23 - Linda Tanner, Tom England, Kevin Landwer-Johan; p 36 - One dead president.

A CIP catalogue record of this book is available from the British Library.

All rights reserved. No part of this publication may be reproduced, stored in a retrieval system, or transmitted, in any form or by any means, electronic, mechanical, photocopying, recording or otherwise, without the prior permission of the publishers.

The rights of David Orme to be identified as the author and of Martin Roy to be identified as the illustrator of this Work have been asserted by them in accordance with sections 77 and 78 of the Copyright, Design and Patents Act 1988.

page 5

page 25

Snakes: The Facts

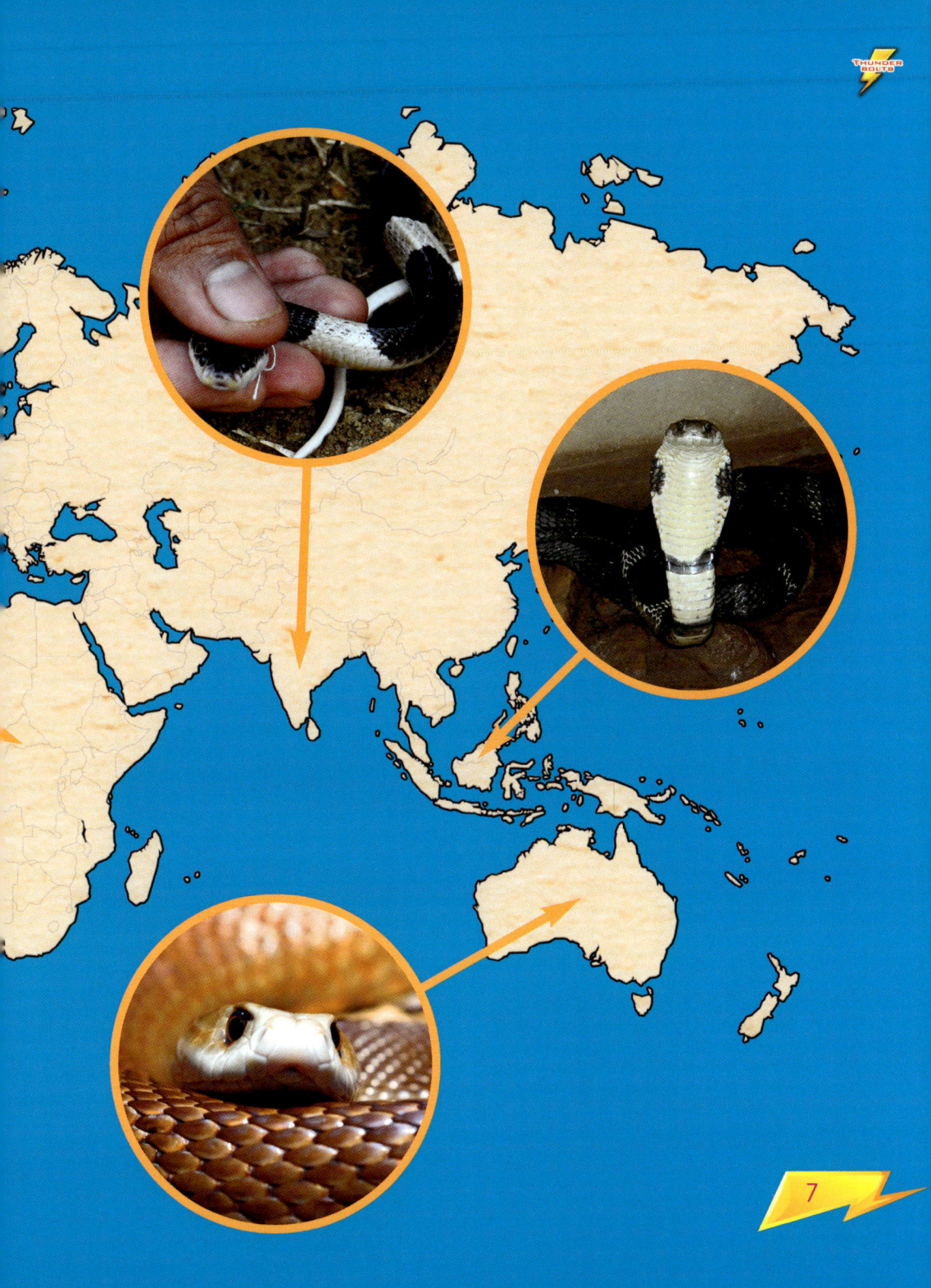

3.5m

6.6m

3.0m

16

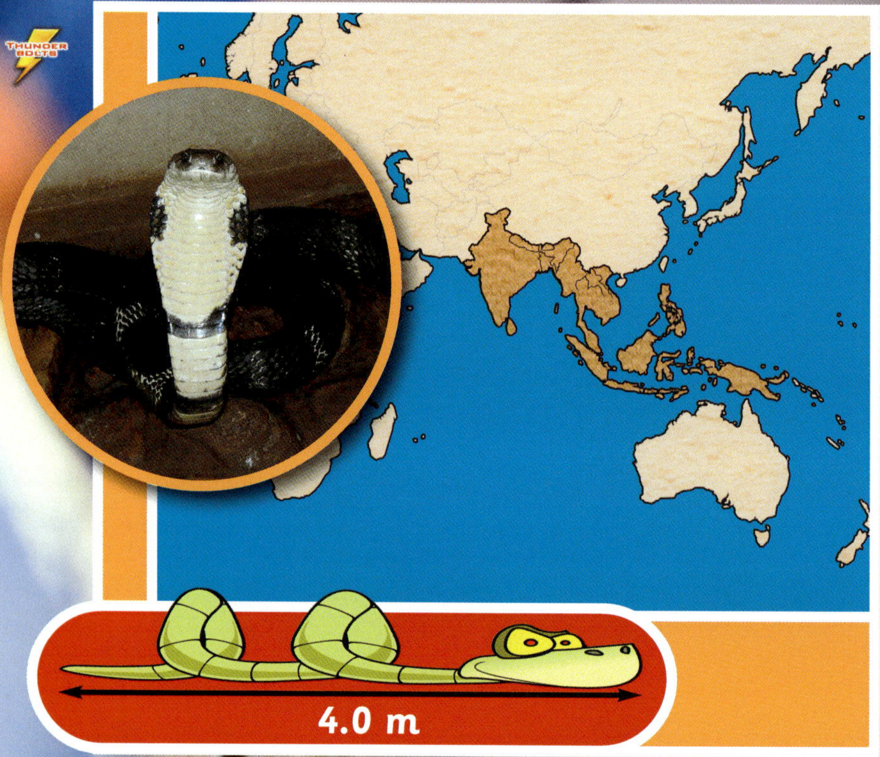

4.0 m

1.5m